A Griffin Day Publication

Play Valley Kids
www.playvalleykids.com
Published by Griffin Day Publishing
8 Cashmere Court
Derrimut Vic 3030

Printed by C&C Printing
Graphic design by Caroline Vendramin

Printed in China.

ISBN 9780646525853

Kick it to me
Jack plays soccer

Written by B.M. Harper
Illustrated by Benjamin Sullivan

Jack was happy.
He was happy because
he was walking in the
park with his dad.

As they walked together, they started to hear loud whistles and kids shouting.

'It sounds like they are having fun. Can we have a look please Dad? PLEEEASE?'
'Of course we can little Jack,' and they walked together until they found a big park, with open spaces and kids running around and they were all wearing uniforms.

'Where are we, Dad?' asked Jack.
Jack's dad looked down and smiled.

Do you know what they had found?
'This is the Play Valley Kids soccer pitch.'

Suddenly a big round ball as big as Jack's head
came rolling over and stopped at Jack's feet.
And then the boys and girls came running
over chasing the ball. They were all very excited.

The ball came to rest right at Jack's feet.

But Jack didn't know how.

Instead, when he went to kick the ball, he swung with his foot as hard as he could, but missed and fell over.

'Ooops,' said Jack, all embarrassed.
Then one of the boys came running
over and got it himself.

Jack felt frustrated that he had looked
so silly in front of the bigger kids.

'Can we go home now Dad?' asked Jack.

'Of course we can.'

Back home Jack was sitting on the couch thinking about what happened in the park. Then, suddenly his dad appeared with a big grin and something behind his back.

'Guess what I have behind my back little Jack?' asked his dad.

Is it a Soccer ball?
YES

'Would you like to learn how to kick a soccer ball, Jack' asked dad.
'Ok, said Jack, still a little unsure of himself. And off they went to the park to practise.

Jack was standing holding the ball, waiting to learn how to play soccer.

'Jack,' said his dad, 'you don't use your hands in soccer. You use your feet. It's called dribbling.'

'Ha ha ha,' laughed Jack.

'No son, you dribble the ball with your feet, not dribble on the ball with your mouth,' and he laughed too.

Dribbling

For more tips on dribbling go to playvalleykids.com

'Let's do a drill, so you can practice. There are three tips I want you to remember:

1. Watch the ball

2. Keep the ball close to your feet

3. Keep your body forward.'

So Jack took the soccer ball and dribbled it around as his dad had said, keeping the ball at his feet and watching it closely.

'Good dribbling', said Dad. And Jack smiled and stuck his chest out. Proud of how good he was.

1. Watch the ball

2. Kick it with the inside of your foot

'Now let's learn another good soccer skill.'

3. Keep your body forward

Passing

For more tips on passing go to playvalleykids.com

'Because soccer's a team game, passing is very important.'
'How do I pass the ball Dad?' asked Jack.
'There are three tips I want you to remember when you're passing the ball, little Jack.'

'Let's practise passing to each other little Jack. Here, pass the ball to me and I'll pass it back.'

Can you remember the three tips for passing?

2. Inside of the foot

1. Step into it

3. Follow through

'Good passing Jack, now you'll be able to kick the ball to the bigger kids.'

Trapping

For more tips on trapping go to playvalleykids.com

'When the ball is rolling towards you, you need to stop it. Stopping the ball with your feet is called trapping and there are three tips you need to know.'

'Here you go Jack, do you remember the tips for trapping?'

1. Watch the ball

2. Get behind the ball

3. Watch the ball all the way to your foot and stop it softly

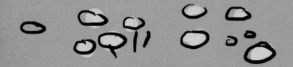

'Good trapping little Jack. Now you can dribble, pass and trap the ball.'

'Ok little Jack' said his dad, 'the next part is the tricky part, let's put it ALL together'.

Jack passed his dad the ball, then, when it came back, he trapped it, and dribbled it close to goal.

He was about to shoot.

'WAIT!' cried his dad, 'you haven't learnt how to shoot yet.'

But Jack didn't wait. He swung at the ball just like a pass and it rolled into the net.

'I scored a goal Dad, WOO HOO,' yelled Jack with a big smile on his face.

'Good one Jack. We can try it a few more times if you like?'

'Yeah' yelled Jack, proud of what he had done.

After a short while Jack's dad said, 'It's getting dark Jack, we better go home for dinner.'

'Ok, ' said Jack reluctantly. He was having so much fun he didn't ever want to stop.

'Tomorrow we can play together some more if you like.'

'Yippee,' said Jack, now looking forward to getting up in the morning so he could practise dribbling, passing, and trapping some more.

'Thanks for showing me how to play soccer today Dad.'

'No problem, it was fun, wasn't it?'

'Yeah, it was,' said Jack, and together they dribbled the ball all the way home.

A few weeks later they went to the park to practise again and guess what happened? The bigger kids were playing a game together and sure enough, their ball rolled over to Jack.

Before the bigger kids could even say a word,
Jack trapped the rolling ball, dribbled it
forward, then passed it straight to the feet of
the biggest kid.
'Nice pass', he said.

Jack smiled the biggest smile ever. 'That was fantastic,' said Jack's Dad.

Jack no longer felt like a little kid. He could play soccer like the big kids, all thanks to his dad and practice.

Kids love to play

It's in their nature, because play time is fun.

As parents, we have a great opportunity to actively encourage our kids to play sport and to promote to them an active lifestyle to sustain them for life.

For children, the skills learned in their early sporting development, can influence their entire lives. From confidence and fair play, to team work and team spirit - these essential human traits are all part of sporting endeavour.

At Play Valley Kids, we believe that learning good technique as youngsters is very important for good development.

Your child may never play sport professionally, or represent their country, but they will derive so much from the games they play that those ambitions are secondary, even irrelevant. Kids play sports for the fun of it.